There Was an OLD LADY Who Swallowed Some BUGS

Adapted and Illustrated
by Johnette Downing

PELICAN PUBLISHING COMPANY
GRETNA 2010

For Dianne

*The word "Pelican" and the depiction of a pelican
are trademarks of Pelican Publishing Company, Inc.,
and are registered in the U.S. Patent and Trademark Office.*

ISBN 9781589808584

Printed in Singapore
Published by Pelican Publishing Company, Inc.
1000 Burmaster Street, Gretna, Louisiana 70053

There was an old lady
who swallowed a spider
that wiggled and jiggled
and tickled inside **her.**

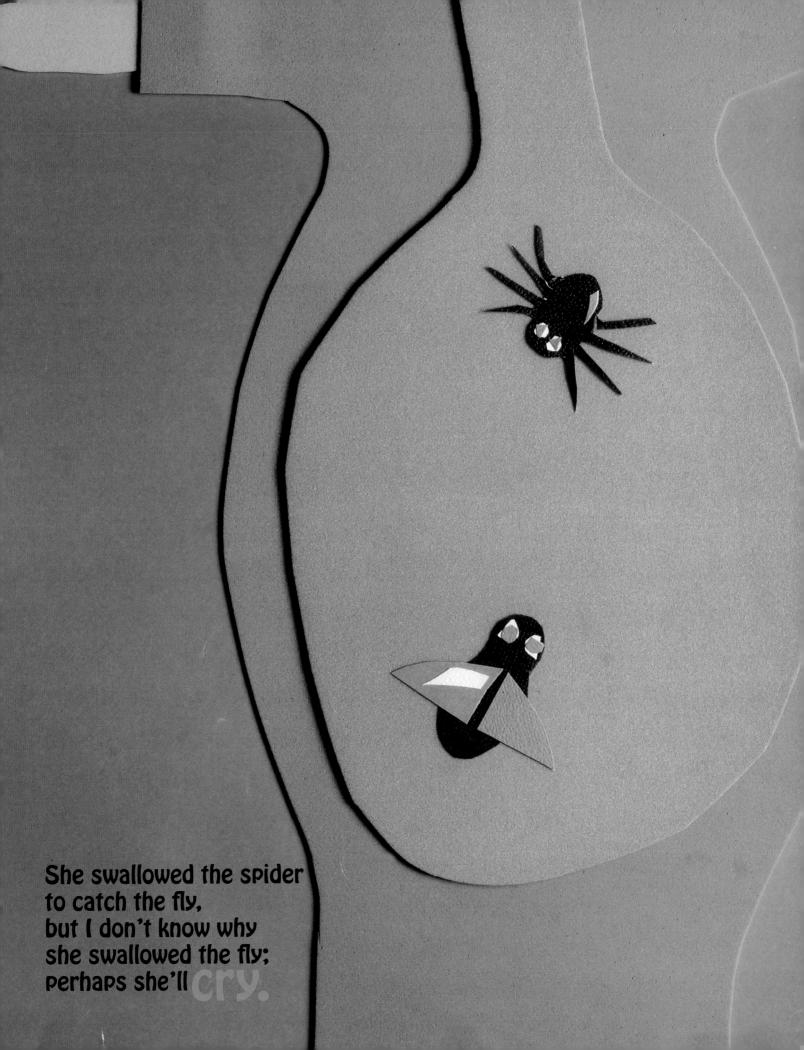

She swallowed the spider
to catch the fly,
but I don't know why
she swallowed the fly;
perhaps she'll cry.

There was an old lady
who swallowed a flea.
Golly gee,
she swallowed a **flea?**

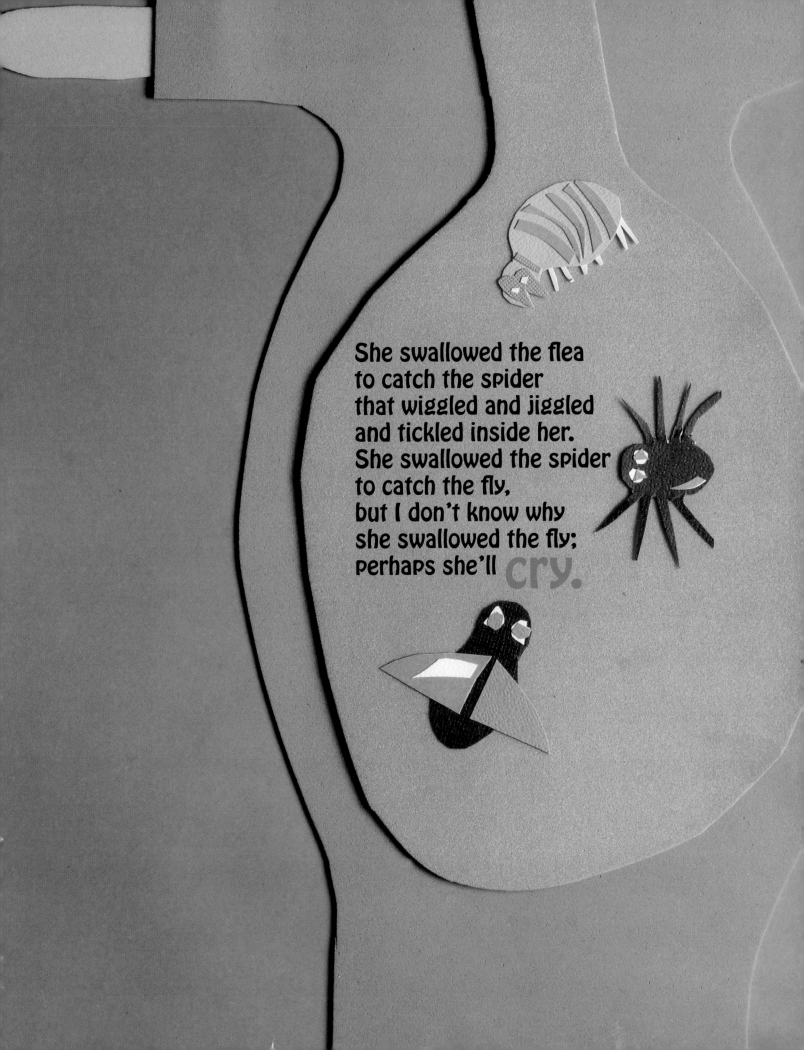

She swallowed the flea
to catch the spider
that wiggled and jiggled
and tickled inside her.
She swallowed the spider
to catch the fly,
but I don't know why
she swallowed the fly;
perhaps she'll cry.

There was an old lady
who swallowed an ant.
She was on a rant when
she swallowed that
ant.

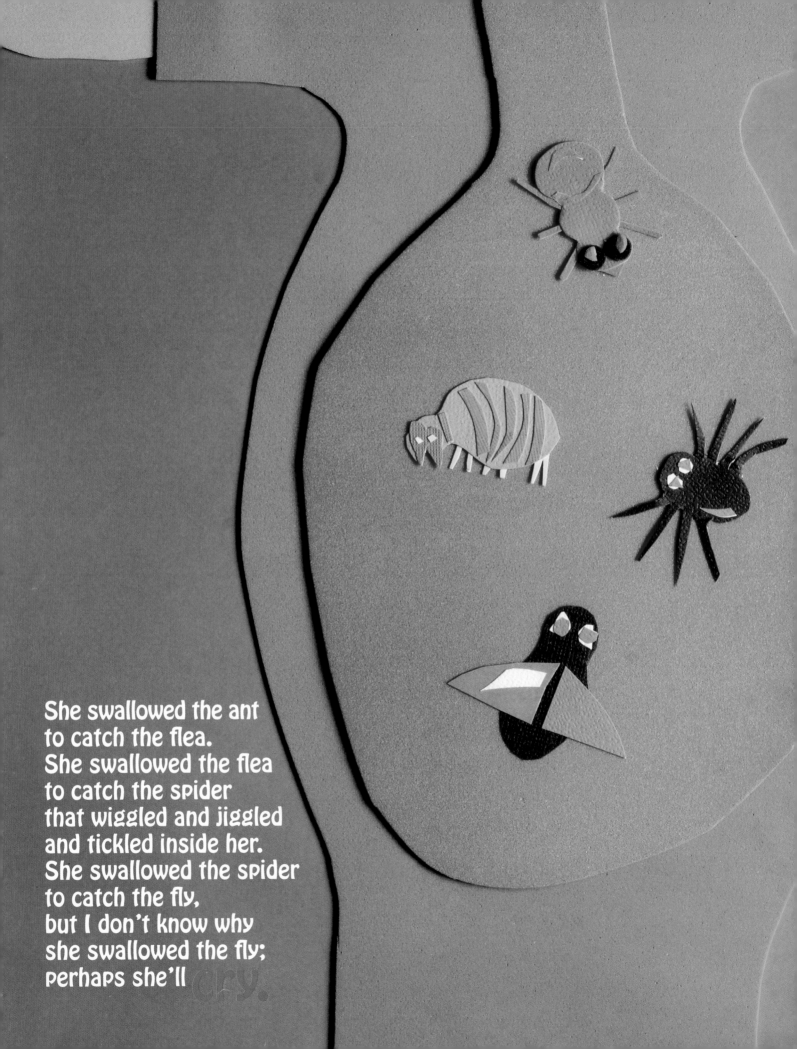

She swallowed the ant
to catch the flea.
She swallowed the flea
to catch the spider
that wiggled and jiggled
and tickled inside her.
She swallowed the spider
to catch the fly,
but I don't know why
she swallowed the fly;
perhaps she'll

There was an old lady
who swallowed a slug.
It's a tasty little bug.
She swallowed the slug.

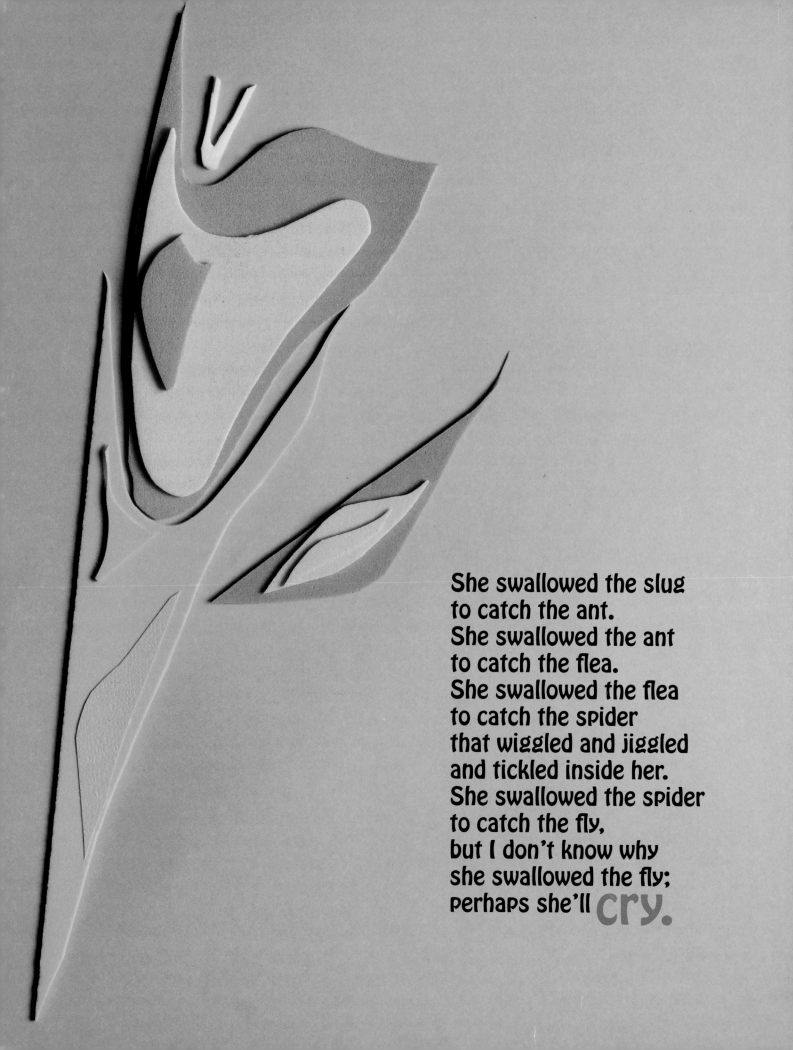

She swallowed the slug
to catch the ant.
She swallowed the ant
to catch the flea.
She swallowed the flea
to catch the spider
that wiggled and jiggled
and tickled inside her.
She swallowed the spider
to catch the fly,
but I don't know why
she swallowed the fly;
perhaps she'll cry.

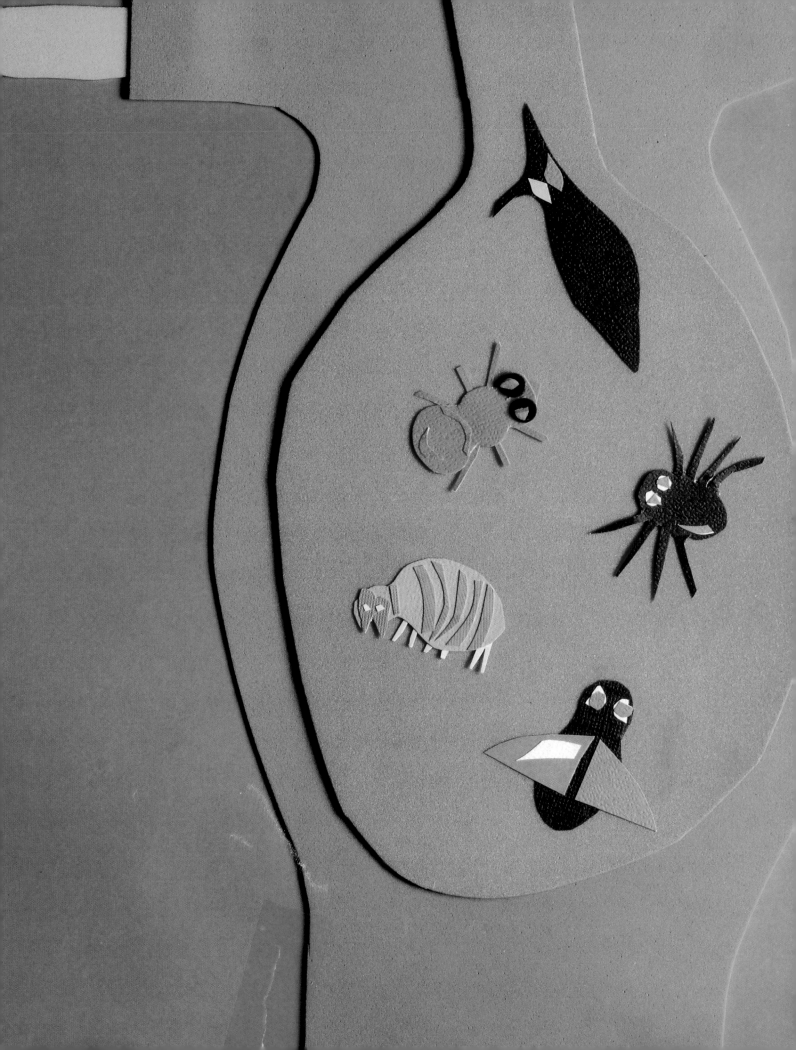

There was an old lady
who swallowed a worm.
It wiggled and squirmed
when she swallowed that worm.

She swallowed the worm
to catch the slug.
She swallowed the slug
to catch the ant.
She swallowed the ant
to catch the flea.
She swallowed the flea
to catch the spider
that wiggled and jiggled
and tickled inside her.
She swallowed the spider
to catch the fly,
but I don't know why
she swallowed the fly;
perhaps she'll cry.

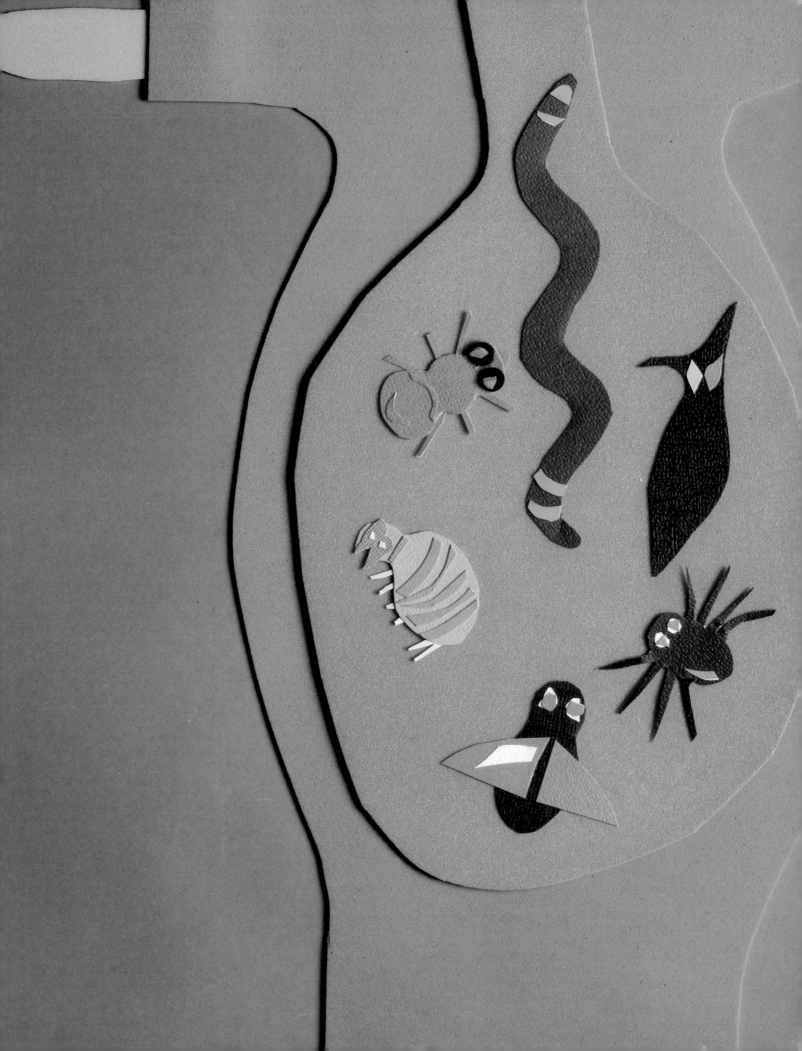

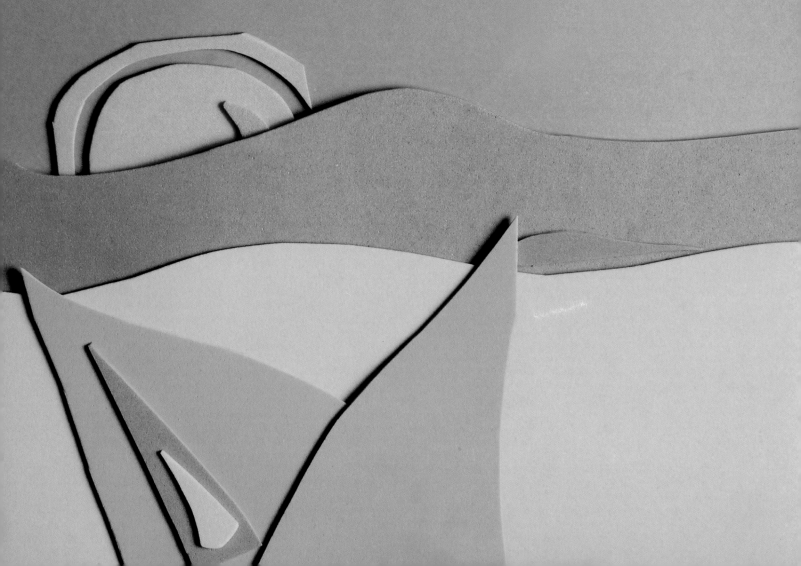

There was an old lady
who swallowed a mosquito.
Well, it was eating her burrito,
so she swallowed the mosquito.

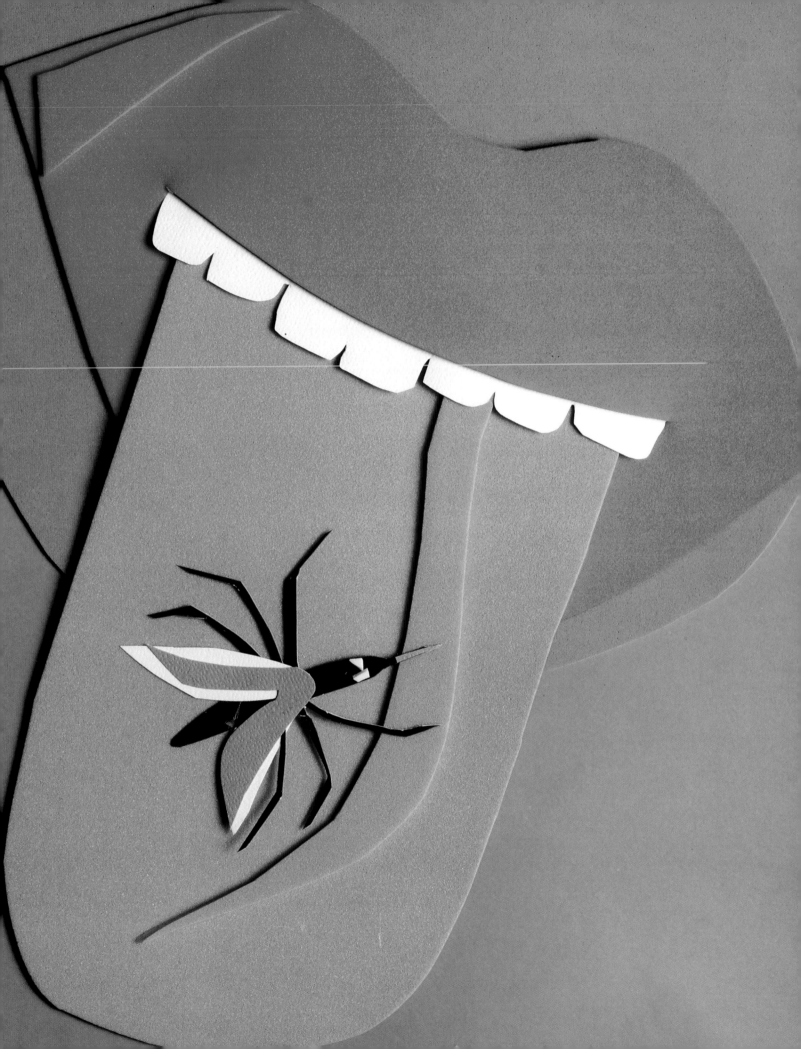

She swallowed the mosquito
to catch the worm.
She swallowed the worm
to catch the slug.
She swallowed the slug
to catch the ant.
She swallowed the ant
to catch the flea.
She swallowed the flea
to catch the spider
that wiggled and jiggled
and tickled inside her.
She swallowed the spider
to catch the fly,
but I don't know why
she swallowed the fly;
perhaps she'll cry.

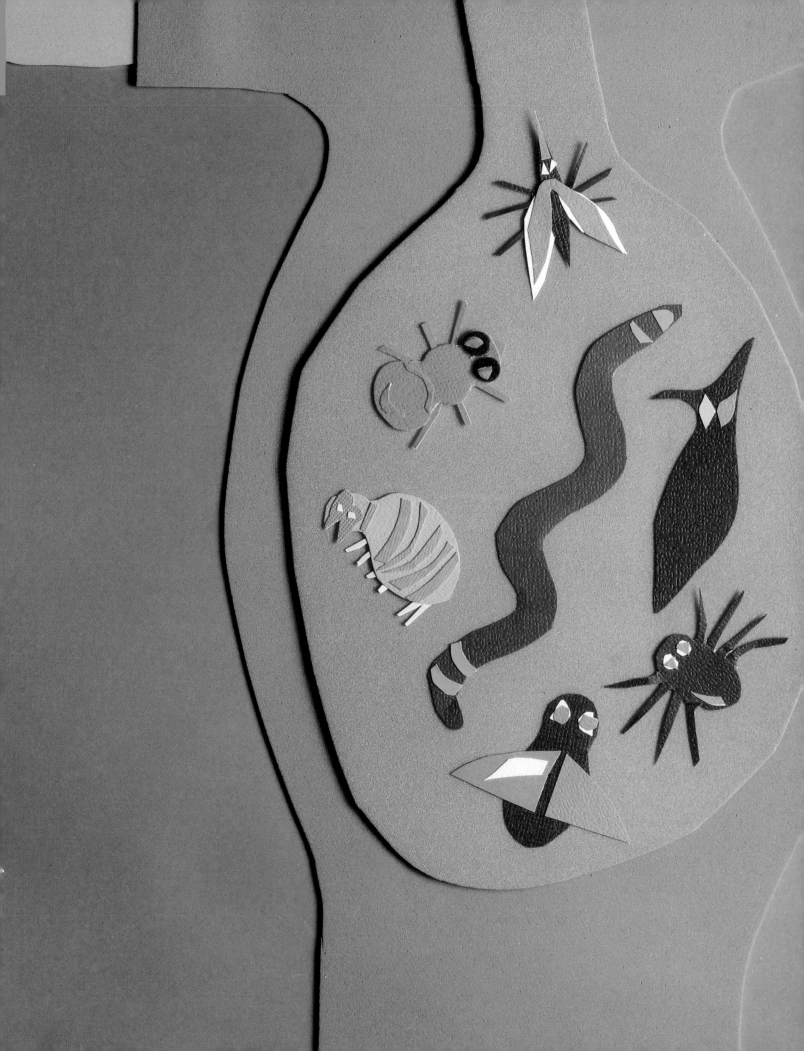

There was an old lady
who swallowed a roach.
She liked them poached.
She swallowed a roach.

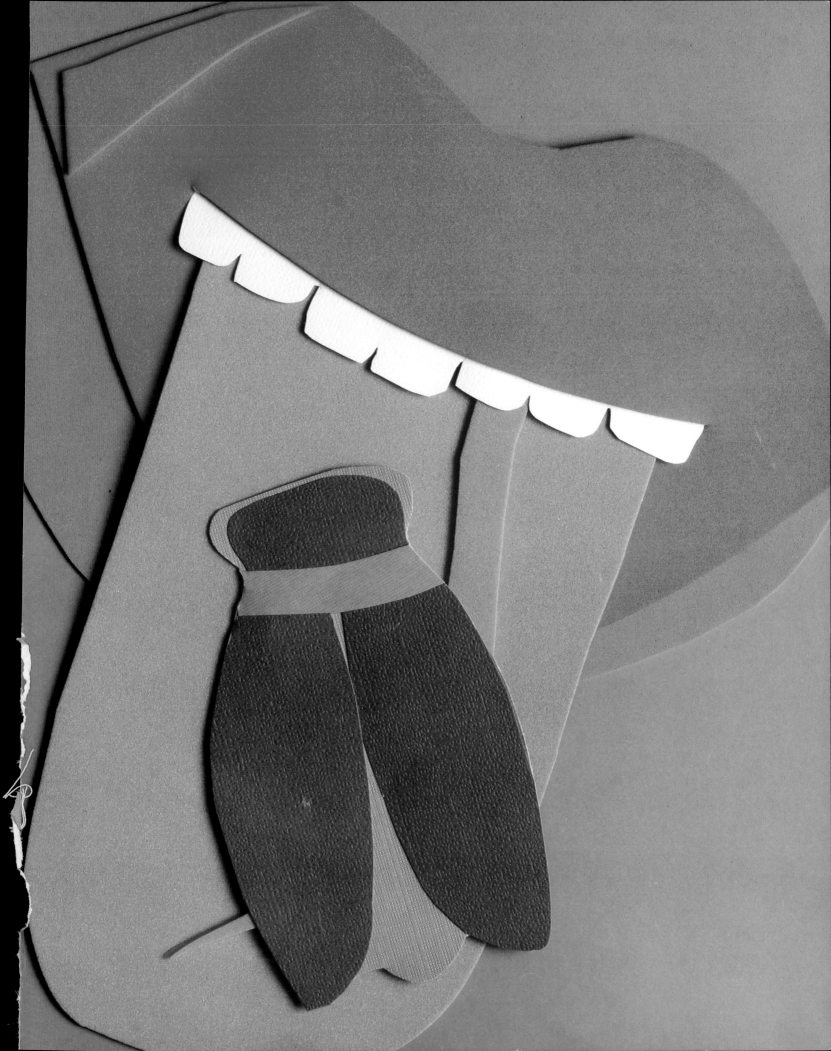

She swallowed the roach
to catch the mosquito.
She swallowed the mosquito
to catch the worm.
She swallowed the worm
to catch the slug.
She swallowed the slug
to catch the ant.
She swallowed the ant
to catch the flea.
She swallowed the flea
to catch the spider
that wiggled and jiggled
and tickled inside her.
She swallowed the spider
to catch the fly,
but I don't know why
she swallowed the fly;
perhaps she'll cry.

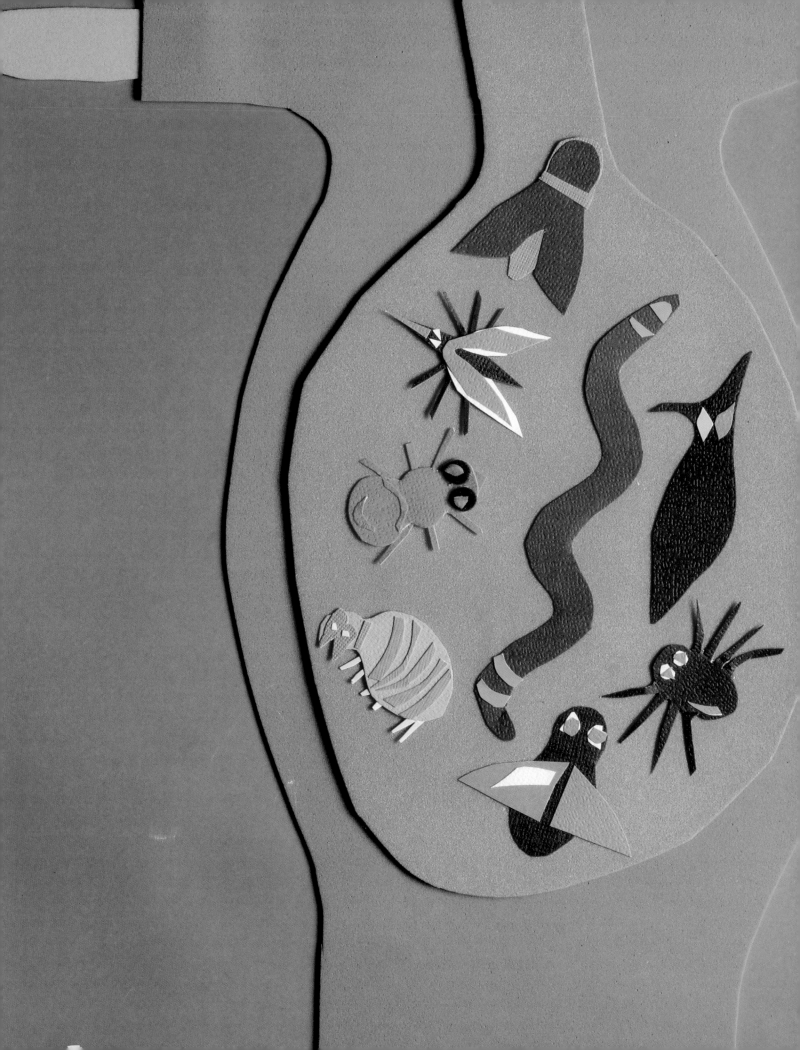

When she was full,
her tummy was **tight.**

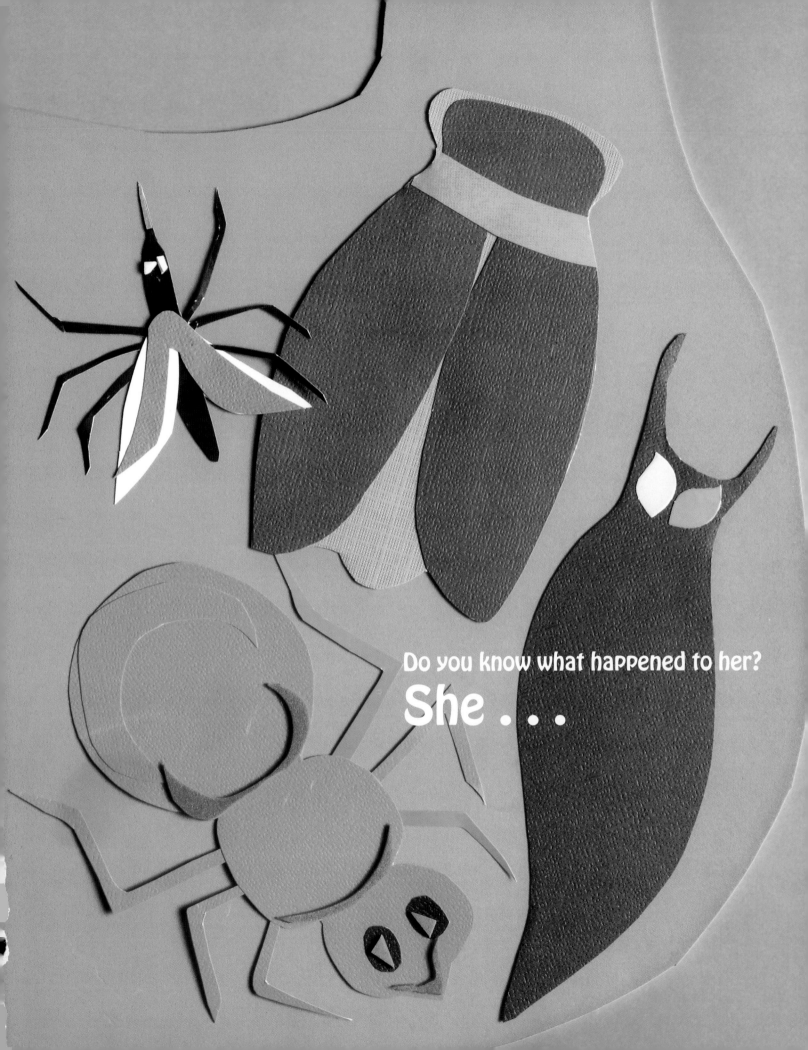

Do you know what happened to her?
She . . .

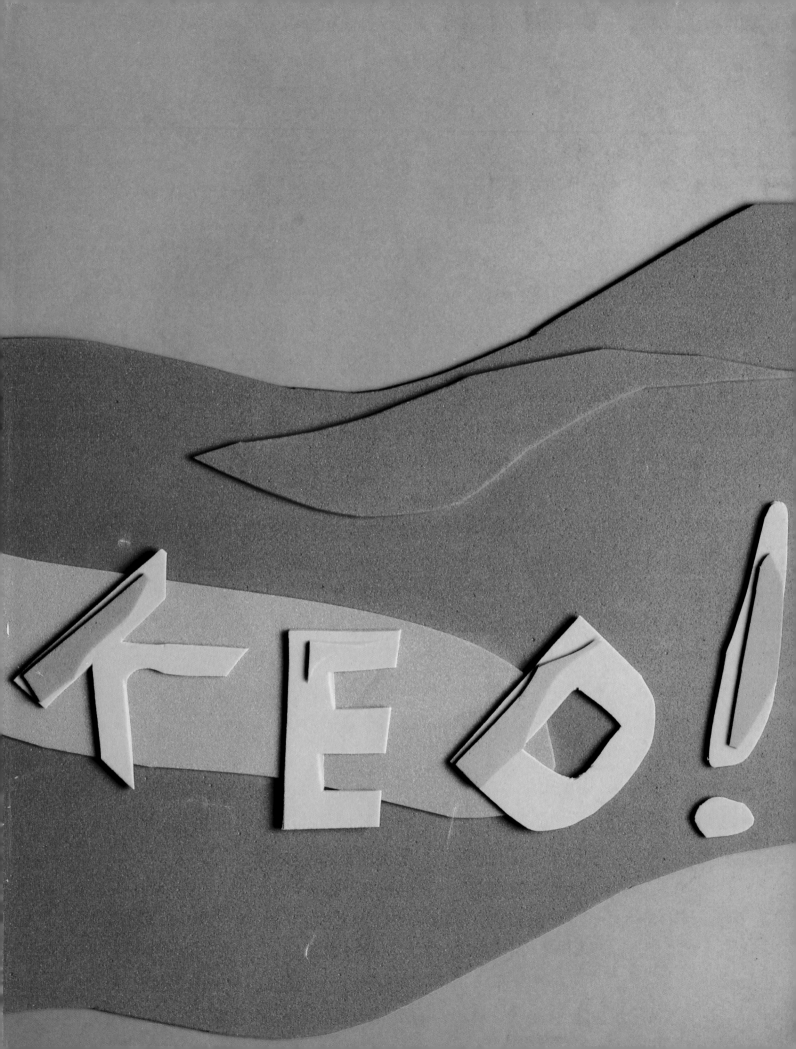